The Adventures of Tallulah Gosh

TallULah aND
The TeeNSTaRS

Acknowledgements

A big thank you to Campbell Brown and Alison McBride and the team at Black & White Publishing. Robert Kirby and Charlotte Knee at United Agents. An extra special thank you to Muntsa Vicente for her amazing illustrations. My husband Stephen for listening to me going on and on about Tallulah (and everything else). My sisters Margaret and Kathleen who still let me borrow their stuff ... And last but not least, thanks to my gorgeous baba – my inspiration.

The Adventures of Tallulah Gosh

TaLLULah aND The TeeNSTaRS

cLaRe gROgaN

BLACK & WHITE PUBLISHING

First published 2008
by Black & White Publishing Ltd
29 Ocean Drive, Edinburgh EH6 6JL

1 3 5 7 9 10 8 6 4 2   08 09 10 11 12

ISBN: 978 1 84502 228 0

Typeset by RefineCatch Limited, Bungay, Suffolk
Printed and bound by Norhaven A/S, Denmark

For Mum and Dad

'Aw, Mum! I'm right in the middle of my new hit.'

chapTeR oNe

Me

WOW! The noise was deafening. The audience roared. Finally, I was in the spotlight. Me. Tallulah. From Tallulah and the TeenStars. Finally I'd made it and it was brilliant! But as I stepped forward to the microphone to announce our next song and brand new single, 'Baby I Don't Bebo', I was rudely interrupted.

'Teresa! Hurry up! Your tea's on the table!' It was Mum from downstairs in the kitchen.

'Aw, Mum! I'm right in the middle of my new hit.'

'OK, Britney. I'll just give your tea to your Dad.'

'It's Tallulah, not Britney,' I said under my breath, then shouted back, 'I'll be there in a minute.'

With that, the magic spell was broken. Super-glamorous Tallulah was plain old Teresa again and I was standing in the middle of my half-untidy bedroom, staring in the mirror and posing outrageously with my gleaming Fender JagStang guitar. Bought with my very own money.

I can still remember every single odd job I did around the neighbourhood to raise the money, including de-nitting next door's cat. UGH! And I'll never forget going to the guitar shop on my thirteenth birthday with my best friend Elizabeth to buy it. And, of course, I had to have the same guitar as Betty, lead singer with The Bee Stings. It was only the third time Elizabeth and I had been allowed to go into town together.

Now, I should explain that my bedroom was only half untidy because I share the room with my big sister Patti. And she's *so* annoying. A real goody two-shoes and a bit of a tidy-freak. Patti keeps her side of the room scarily spotless. She even has her side of the wardrobe colour-coded. Hard to believe that anyone could have all their white clothes at one end of the rail, all their black clothes at the other end and shades of grey in the middle. Scary!

I'm the complete opposite. I can never find time to tidy my half of the room, which drives Patti mad. But I'm far too busy touring the world with my fabulous band Tallulah and the TeenStars. What with the TV appearances and making the new album and the new vid –

'Teresa, I'm not going to call you again,' Mum

bellowed. 'It's lasagne and your Dad's looking hungry!'

Actually, lasagne's my favourite so I raced downstairs to the kitchen three at a time. Patti and my biggest sister Maggie, who's at college doing a beauty course *and has her own room*, had just started their tea but Dad had already finished his. He's *so* embarrassing. Eats like a pig! He was even staring at *my* plate when I got there until I said, 'Forget it, Dad. It's mine!' Sometimes living in the Gordon house is like a fight for survival.

We don't always sit down to eat tea together but Mum insists we do at least once a week. Patti was looking less grumpy than usual after her lasagne so I asked, 'Is Gary coming over tonight, cos I need to ask him about the chords to …'

'Forget it, squirt. Gary's coming to see *me*. You've already had your guitar lesson this week and I don't want you hanging around us. OK?' She didn't even bother to look at me.

Gary is Patti's boyfriend. He's eighteen, has his own car, is at college doing a music-type thing and he's my guitar teacher. It really gets on Patti's nerves that Gary helps me but it goes down very well with Mum and Dad. They didn't think that Patti should be going out with an older boy who's already left school but now they seem to think he's OK.

Life in the Gordon family is very, very normal. Like any family, on any street, anywhere. Without the band, life would just be *too* dull.

After tea, Elizabeth arrived and I couldn't wait to play her my new song. She didn't think up songs on her own but she always wanted to hear what I'd done. As usual, she'd lugged her bass guitar over. She'd got it from her cousin who'd decided to buy a new one. We went up to my room and I got the JagStang ready for action.

Then the trouble started.

Patti arrived at the door shouting, 'Right, you two, out now! Gary will be here in a minute.'

'No way,' I said. 'It's my room too!'

But she wasn't backing down. Especially not now that Gary had just arrived.

'I mean it. Get lost!' said Patti, menacingly.

That's the thing about sisters. People think they're so nice but they don't see what I see. The *real* big sister.

I tried pleading with her. 'Patti, we're having our band practice here and we don't have anywhere else to go.'

'Teresa, you don't even have a band and even if you did it would probably be the worst band in the world,' said Patti.

Elizabeth was just looking embarrassed as she

Life in the Gordon family is very, very normal

always did in front of boys ... any boys ... all boys. Even boys on the other side of the street!

'We do so have a band!' I yelled back. 'We're called Tallulah and the TeenStars and we're brilliant.'

'Yeah right. In your dreams, loser!' said Patti,

making an 'L' shape with her fingers and trying to look cool.

'We do have a band, *actually*,' I said icily.

'Oh really?' said Patti, with a glint in her eye. 'So I suppose your pathetic little band will be entering the school talent contest in a few weeks then?'

'As a matter of fact we are!' I exclaimed.

The words were out of my mouth before I could stop them. I'd said it and there was no going back now. I looked at Elizabeth and her mouth was opening and closing but there was no sound coming out. She looked like a fish!

'Yeah, right!' said Patti as she shoved us out of the room and slammed the door. Finally, Elizabeth managed to speak and it all came out in a torrent. '*Teresa you're mad there's no way we can enter a talent contest in such a short time with a band that doesn't exist and you'll just have to tell Patti you were making it up and say sorry and tell her you weren't serious and we don't really have a band and ... and ...*'

'*No way!*' I yelled, feeling a bit less brave than I sounded. 'In two weeks TALLULAH AND THE TEENSTARS are going to be on that stage no matter what it takes.'

I looked at Elizabeth. She'd turned a funny colour and looked like she was going to be sick. I knew exactly how she felt.

CHAPTER TWO

Tallulah and the TeenStars

After the most amazing weekend of my life – planning everything with the band – school seemed pretty dull on a wet Monday morning. I thought the maths lesson would *never* end and when the bell went at lunchtime, I dragged Elizabeth off to the art room for our very first *real band meeting*.

'Right,' I said to her, 'we've got a talent contest to win.'

Elizabeth looked scared. 'I've told you, Teresa, this really isn't a good idea. There's no way you can do it.'

'No way *we* can do it,' I corrected her. 'But I think you're wrong. All we need to do is get a plan in place and get ourselves organised.'

'It doesn't matter how organised we are. The whole school is still going to laugh at us,' said Elizabeth.

I must say it hurt a bit that she said that, but I suppose she did have a point. But this was our *big* chance to show everyone who we really were.

'Right,' I said briskly, 'I've brought along the rules to the contest and all we have to do is learn one really brilliant song for the first round and, if we get through to the final the following week, we'll need another one. Surely we can do that!'

Elizabeth looked like she'd cheered up a bit now so I said, 'Come on, let's get the poster designed for the auditions.'

We only had half an hour left before English but I think we did a great job getting the poster ready, including the final touches in purple glitter pen.

'Are you sure your Mum and Dad won't mind us using the garage, Teresa?' Elizabeth asked.

'They go out every Friday night, so they won't even know,' I assured her.

Just then, the bell went for English and I had a great idea.

'Elizabeth, you go back to class and tell Mr Lironi I'll be a few minutes late. Make up any excuse you like. I'll wait until the coast is clear and put the poster up on the noticeboard so that no-one will know who Tallulah and the TeenStars are. Until the auditions. Go on then, go.'

Elizabeth trudged off to class looking slightly glum again and I went off to the toilets to wait until everything was quiet.

The main noticeboard was outside the assembly

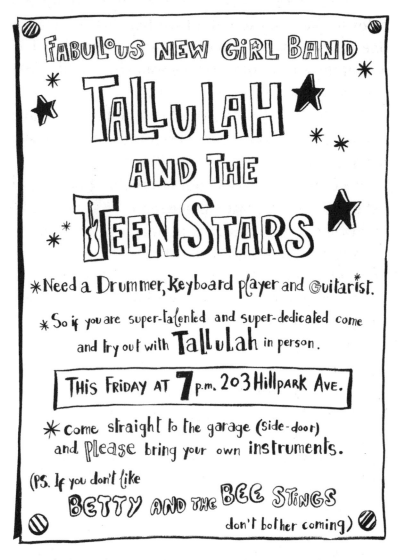

FABULOUS NEW GIRL BAND

TALLULAH
AND THE
TEENSTARS

*Need a Drummer, Keyboard player and Guitarist.

* So if you are super-talented and super-dedicated come and try out with **Tallulah** in person.

THIS FRIDAY AT **7** p.m. 203 Hillpark Ave.

* Come straight to the garage (side-door) and **please** bring your own **instruments**.

(P.S. If you don't like
BETTY AND THE BEE STINGS
don't bother coming)

We only had half an hour left before English but I think we did a great job getting the poster ready

hall and a bit too close to the staff room for comfort. From the door to the toilets I could just see the last teachers and pupils scurrying off to class and a minute later the whole school seemed like it was deserted.

I snuck out of the door and ran over to the noticeboard, whipped out the poster from my bag and stuck it up right in the middle with four purple thumbtacks. I stood back for a moment and realised that there was a big smile on my face. It looked brilliant!

When I finally got to class I was nearly five minutes late.

'Feeling better, Teresa?' said Mr Lironi.

'Yes, thank you, sir,' I mumbled and shot Elizabeth a grateful glance.

For the rest of that week, Elizabeth and I walked 'casually' past the noticeboard about every five minutes during break time. I was desperate to see who was looking at our poster but there never seemed to be anyone there at all. Nobody paid any attention to it and it might as well have been invisible. There was no talk in the girls' toilets, no mention of it in the cold-lunch corridor, and not even a single word at the bus stop about the amazing new band.

'It's official, we're completely invisible, even

when we're not being ourselves. Even our fabulous other-selves are invisible,' I said to Elizabeth.

It was a very, *very* long week and by the time Friday arrived I was sure there was only going to be one TeenStar at the talent contest, although I wasn't even sure that Elizabeth would turn up.

To cheer myself up, I decided to 'borrow' one of Patti's dresses. She has loads in her colour-coded side of the wardrobe so I was sure she wouldn't miss one.

Just then, my mobile rang.

'Hey T, what are you going to wear?' a surprisingly upbeat Elizabeth asked. 'I've decided on my new black shorts, with footless tights and my yellow and black striped T-shirt and my black glittery wedges. So I'm just checking you're not going to wear your wedges?'

Elizabeth was developing a passion for fashion. School had a strict uniform policy, so you could only experiment out of school, which we both loved to do, but usually just in our bedrooms.

'Cool,' I said. A clothes conversation always cheers Elizabeth up. Unless, of course, she's having a clothes crisis. 'I'm borrowing that grey flowery prom dress that Patti wore to The Lavenders gig that we weren't allowed to go to last month, with my pale blue Converse boots.'

'Hey T, what are you going to wear?'

'Mmm, that'll look great. She doesn't mind you borrowing her dress then?' asked El.

'She doesn't actually know, which makes borrowing it a bit easier,' I replied, giggling nervously.

'OK, see you around half six,' Elizabeth said, giggling as well now.

I couldn't wait for 7 o'clock to come. I was feeling really excited, really nervous and was wondering if I should put out some snacks. I couldn't wait to find out who my TEENSTARS were going to be. I knew they were out there, but would anyone *really* turn up?

chapter three

Garage Band

The doorbell finally went at quarter to seven. Elizabeth peered out from behind her bass guitar. She looked pale but managed a wee smile.

'Sorry I'm late,' she said sheepishly.

'Come on, Elizabeth, it's not going to be that bad! Let's go and set up.'

Elizabeth nodded. She seemed to have lost the power of speech again as we headed to the garage.

Elizabeth is small for her age and I used to tease her that the only reason I wanted her to be my friend was because she was the only girl in the class smaller than me. I know it's not that funny a joke, but Elizabeth always laughs and never takes offence. But if anyone else makes fun of our height, well, that's altogether a different story and very annoying. Our littleness unites us in lots of little ways. She was setting up her amp next to the old doorless fridge in our garage and when she lifted her bass guitar over her head she looked even tinier than usual. She still looked as white as a sheet and I hoped she wasn't going to pass out.

Just as I was tuning up my guitar and looking, I think, pretty good in Patti's dress, there was a knock at the door. 'Come in!' I shouted nervously.

The door opened slowly and … I just couldn't believe it! It was none other than Lawrence Aitken, better known to us as Sir Acne No-mates. He's basically posh and spotty with no friends.

'Teresa Gordon!' he said. 'What are you doing

'Teresa Gordon!' he said. 'What are you doing here?'

here?' He didn't even look at me as he pushed past me looking for Tallulah. 'I'm here to meet Tallulah, where is she?'

'She's not here yet,' I said, bottling it. 'Anyway, she only wants girls in the band.'

'Well, I'll just have to remind her that's against the law,' said Sir Acne. Add know-all to the list of reasons that nobody likes Lawrence. 'Anyway, once she hears me play she'll soon change her mind.'

He was carrying what looked like a suitcase and out of it he produced a French Horn, (which is a trumpet-like thing), a giant box of cuppa-soup and a stuffed rat.

Elizabeth and I looked at each other wide-eyed, realising he was actually totally MAD.

'Just go, Lawrence. Tallulah's just called. She's not coming – her hamster died,' I said, practically pushing him out of the garage door. He trudged off down the path looking less than pleased, taking his suitcase, his soup and his rat with him.

Just then I spotted Poppy What's-Her-Name unloading a drum-kit from the back of her Dad's Scenic. Poppy is just about the quietest girl in the whole year. She's not unfriendly, she's just really shy or something.

'Is Tallulah here?' Poppy asked in a whisper. 'I've come to audition for the band.'

I stepped forward to help her with her stuff. 'I'm Tallulah. Do you want to set your kit up beside the running machine, over there?'

Poppy looked at me, but didn't say what she was obviously thinking. Which is *how on earth can YOU be Tallulah?!?* Maybe it was just as well the quietest girl in the school had turned up!

As Poppy was setting up, Hayley MacIntosh arrived, with her keyboard. She's in the school orchestra and plays the piano and Elizabeth told me she doesn't Bebo. She'd also brought another girl along who I didn't recognise. The other girl was called Louisa and she plays guitar. Turns out she goes to another school but heard about the band through Hayley.

By now it was already quarter past seven and it looked like no-one else would be turning up. 'OK,' I shouted over the noise. 'Does anyone know the Bee Stings' song 'Roller Coaster Casualty'?'

They all nodded.

'Let's give it a go then, shall we? One, two, three, FOUR!'

I have to admit I thought the only casualty when we started to play would be the mangled song but even though it was so loud I couldn't hear myself think, it really wasn't too bad for a first go. We lost it completely at the B section but managed to get it back again for the end chorus. It was brilliant! Incredible!

Until ...

'TERESA GORDON!!!. What on *earth* do you think you are playing at? We can hear you from the bottom of the street!' It was Mum, standing at the garage door, looking just about as purple as our poster.

I'd never heard such a deafening silence after Mum shouted. For what seemed like ages, you could hear a pin drop, even though my ears were ringing.

'Right,' said Mum. 'Out of here, all of you'

Then Patti arrived, screaming like a banshee. 'Teresa, *who said you could wear my dress*? I'm going out in ten minutes and I've been looking everywhere for it, you stupid eejit.'

'Right,' said Mum. 'Out of here, all of you! Teresa, tell your friends to go home and meet me and your father in the kitchen *in* two minutes. *Do you hear me?*' The entire street could hear her – talk about noisy! I could see where Patti got it from!

I nodded dumbly in response and, with that, Mum stormed out of the garage.

'OK, everyone,' I said. 'Only two weeks to the talent contest. See you all next week for our first official rehearsal as the TeenStars. Welcome to the band!'

And on that note, I headed to the kitchen to face the music!

ChaPTeR FOUR

Falling Out

I was lying in bed, wide awake, staring up at the ceiling and I couldn't help but smile to myself even though I'd just had the most *colossal* telling off from Mum and Dad. Well, actually, it was mostly from Mum.

Dad seemed slightly amused about it all and even made the point that all successful garage bands have to start somewhere. And it's usually in the garage. That just made Mum go even more mental and Dad got one of her amazingly scary 'death glares' before she stomped off. Maybe I should have waited a bit before asking them to call me Tallulah instead of Teresa from now on!

It was obvious that Mum was already in a *very* bad mood. They'd turned up unexpectedly from their fancy dinner party because the hostess's three-year-old son had projectile vomited all over Mum's new dress just as dinner was being served.

Despite the fallout, it had been an incredible evening

According to Dad, the carrot soup starter really lost its appeal after that.

And as for Patti, she got over her 'where's my dress' meltdown pretty quickly and decided to wear something else anyway! Patti's like that. She blows up like a volcano and all you can do is stand as far back as possible. Then she calms down just as quickly and moves on to the next thing that'll make her explode.

Our oldest sister Maggie is the complete opposite. She's slim and pretty and looks like butter wouldn't melt in her mouth but you cross her at your peril. She's a bit like an elephant and never forgets *anything* but it's always the stuff you wish she'd forget. When you have an argument with her, she'll say something like, 'Yes, but when you were seven, you got so excited that you peed yourself on Christmas morning when you got your new mermaid costume.' Who remembers stuff like that? Only Maggie.

Despite the fallout, it had been an incredible evening, especially with the band. And I reckoned it had come together so brilliantly cos the others were all members of The Bee Stings' official fan club as well. We just seemed to instantly gel. Even El sounded not *too* bad. And I was pretty sure Mum and Dad would calm down and change their minds about the band using the garage for rehearsals.

I was just drifting into one of my favourite fantasies, where I'm on T4 being interviewed about the band's forthcoming world tour, when the familiar beep beep of a text message brought me back to reality. It was from Elizabeth and said, 'we'll show them talent! we just need to sort out poppy's dress sense and there will be no stopping us'

I laughed out loud and texted back, 'I quite liked that orange poncho tho. c u tomorrow.'

I switched off my bedside lamp and snuggled deep down under my duvet. I needed to get some sleep as I was determined to be up early (unheard of on a Saturday) to start my campaign to change Mum's mind about us using the garage.

The next morning, the campaign didn't start well.

'Forget it Teresa.' (Typically Mum was blatantly ignoring my request to be called Tallulah!) 'Garages are for cars, not bands.'

'But, Mum! Our garage is half full of junk. The car hasn't been in there since we got it.'

'Teresa, I'm not going to tell you again. The answer is definitely NO.'

Breakfast had got off to a really bad start.

'But Mum, please, where else can we go?'

'If you're serious about the band then you'll find somewhere else. There's no way I'm dealing with complaints from the neighbours just so that you can enter a silly talent contest. And what about your exams? That's what you should be concentrating on, not playing the guitar. And I'm not discussing it any more.'

And with that, Mum left for work. She worked with her sister in their hairdresser's shop, Altered Images, and Saturday was always a busy day for them. She hadn't even drunk the frothy coffee that I'd spent ages making. I'd tried to make it look like a proper 'café' cappuccino and even sprinkled the chocolate on top to make an M shape. What a waste of time!

Feeling a bit flat, I decided to go back to bed.

She hadn't even drunk the frothy coffee that I'd spent ages making

Without the garage, Tallulah and the TeenStars could be history before they'd even happened. I lay on top of my bed feeling totally deflated. Why did everything have to be so difficult?

I was tossing and turning and fidgeting and sighing a lot and really, really loudly, desperately trying to figure out what to do next.

'Oh, for goodness sake, Teresa.' (Patti had obviously decided to ignore my new name as well.) 'There are other garages, you know. Ask the others if they can think of somewhere. Stop being such a drama queen.'

For once, I thought Patti might have a point and texted the TeenStars: 'parents really grumpy. can't play in my garage. any ideas?'

Louisa, the girl I didn't really know, called back almost immediately. 'Hi Tallulah,' she said, getting serious brownie points for being the first person to use my new name. 'My uncle is the janitor at the Hill Street Community Centre. I could ask him if we can use the big hall there.'

'Oh, great!' I said. 'Could you ask him now?'

'No problem,' said Louisa. 'And I think we should start work on our own songs as soon as we can. I've got loads of ideas.'

Ten minutes later, Louisa texted to say it should be OK with her uncle and he was checking it out.

Brilliant news! I think Louisa and I are going to become really good friends.

I called El to tell her but she was on voicemail so I texted to say I'd meet her as usual after her Saturday morning shift in her Dad's fabric shop.

By 12.30 we were in the City Café. We ordered our usual egg mayo rolls followed by pineapple cake and a black coffee each. We'd decided black coffee is quite sophisticated.

'I think that Louisa girl is really cool,' I said. 'She's asked her uncle about us using the community centre to rehearse in.'

Just as I said this, my moby rang. It was an excited Louisa: 'My uncle Pete says we can use the hall. It's free between 4pm and 6pm on a Thursday afternoon and every Saturday morning between 8 and 10.30. And there's a PA system there we can use as well.'

'Wow, it's a bit early on a Saturday, but that's fantastic news. Thanks Louisa.'

As I was nattering away with Louisa, I saw that El was getting a bit fed up. In fact, she was looking *really* cheesed off. So I said 'Ciao' to Louisa and started telling Elizabeth the good news.

Elizabeth interrupted me before I'd barely begun. 'That's great Tallulah, but what am I meant to do, give up my job?'

I'd completely overlooked the fact that El works

in her Dad's shop every Thursday after school and on Saturday mornings. And there was no way her Dad would let her give up her job to play in a band. El looked really fed up.

'El, that's the only time we can practise. I don't know what to do but you really need to be there if you're going to be in the band.'

'Listen, Teresa. You know my Dad wouldn't even let me play in the orchestra on a Saturday morning. He needs me in the shop. There's no way he would let me off to play in a band. I couldn't even ask him – he'd go mad!'

We finished our lunch in silence, both now totally miserable.

Then suddenly Elizabeth stood up. 'Do you know what, Teresa. I'm totally fed up with this whole band thing already. And I think that Louisa girl is totally full of it and she looks like a pig. Which makes you two a perfect pair at the moment.'

Then she turned and walked out making pig noises at me!!

Elizabeth had *never* been so angry with me. Which made me furious too. And after the pig thing there was *no way* we could be best friends. Looked like we were going to be one TeenStar short and just when things were going so well.

chapter five

Change of Heart

'It's me, please call me back El.' It was the fourth time that day I'd left a message for Elizabeth. It was the longest time *ever* we hadn't spoken. I was in my room staring blankly at a history book. I had an essay to hand in tomorrow and hadn't even started it. I looked at my watch and it was past midnight.

What a bore ... I mean, Sundays were always a bit of a drag but this particular Sunday was the worst *ever*. I hadn't even played my guitar because I was too upset to do the one thing that usually cheered me up. I mean, Elizabeth is the best friend ever and I *so* didn't want to fall out with her. I decided I had to make things work with her and the band or else I wasn't sure there was any point in having one – after all, she was the original TeenStar.

I took off my glasses, lay down with my face buried in the pillow and started to cry. Just as well Patti hadn't come to bed yet cos I just couldn't have faced her laughing at me on top of everything else.

The next morning as I got to the bus stop I spotted Elizabeth already waiting there – unusual because it wasn't her stop.

'Listen T, I know I've been a bit of a prat. Fancy a coffee before school?'

'Me too, El. Coffee sounds great,' I replied. 'Let's skip history. I haven't finished my essay anyway.'

'Me neither,' said Elizabeth. 'Starbucks?'

We chit-chatted on the way about stuff, deliberately avoiding the real problem, but when we sat down with our coffees, Elizabeth dropped her bombshell.

'Look T, I'm sorry I completely lost the plot. The thing is I've been thinking and to be honest I've decided I don't really think the band's for me. I want to sell my bass on eBay and buy a sewing machine. I really *really* want to make it on to that TV show *Project Catwalk* and be a fashion designer.'

I sat back in my chair. I couldn't believe what she was saying. 'But Elizabeth, what about all our plans? I can't do it without you. I know we had a fallout yesterday but all I want to do is make things right again and win that talent contest. You just can't *do* this – we *have* to work it out!'

When I'd stopped my rant, El said, 'Listen T. You're a brilliant singer, you can play guitar and you *should* be doing this. But we both know my bass playing isn't really that good and I could never write a song. I thought maybe I'd get better if I practiced but it really hurts my fingers. And if you're going to have a proper band I think you need a proper bass player. Truth is, I'd rather make your stage outfits than play bass in the band. I'm really sorry T, but I just know it's never going to work.'

It looked like Elizabeth had totally made up her mind. In a funny way I was half-relieved – cos her bass playing was all over the place – and half-worried cos what on earth was I going to do now about the talent contest?

'Well that's great El, but what am I going to do about a bass player?' I said.

'Maybe Lawrence has another talent,' El quipped and we both started to laugh. 'But listen, T, you're my best mate and I really don't want to fall out over this. I know you're disappointed but you'll find someone else.'

'OK, El. Looks like I need to find another bass player fast,' I shrugged.

The good thing was that I've never seen her so totally fired up about anything! It sounded like she was really determined to be a fashion designer and she'd even decided on a new fashion name, Eli Le Grande.

We'd been talking for ages and decided it wasn't

worth going in to school before lunchtime. Time for another latte, but as I went up to order – *disaster*! Mr Stevens, our form master, was standing at the counter!

I dashed back to where El was sitting, shushed her to be quiet and dragged her off to the toilets. If he had spotted us, we'd had it.

After five minutes giggling and whispering in the loos, I stuck my head out the door. *Double disaster*! He was standing right there, waiting for us to come out! He frogmarched us back to school and I felt a bit teary at the thought of my Mum and Dad being sent for. I could tell Elizabeth was feeling the same way but nobody said a word. It was just so typical that the one and only time El and I skipped school we'd get caught. Other people seemed to do it all the time and get away with it.

When we finally reached the school gates, Mr Stevens cleared his throat. 'Teresa, Elizabeth, I don't know what you were doing out of school at this time of day and I'm very disappointed with both of you. It's extremely irresponsible of you to behave like that but, as it's so out of character, I have decided not to take any further action this time. But, believe me, if you ever try anything like that again you'll be going straight to see the Head.' And with that he walked off.

Astonished, we hugged each other feeling *totally* relieved.

'Let's decide to *never* fall out again,' El said.

'Absolutely. Never again,' I replied.

We headed to our usual seats in the cold lunch corridor. Hayley and Poppy were there, which was a nice surprise and gave us a chance to have an all-important band meeting. They both already knew the good news – that we had a fabulous new place to rehearse. But not the BAD ...

'OK TeenStars, does anyone know a bass player? El has decided to become a fashion designer and is leaving the band – with my blessing.'

There was a stunned silence and a look of utter

We headed to our usual seats in the cold lunch corridor

panic on Hayley and Poppy's faces. They both looked at Elizabeth and then back at me.

Then Hayley piped up, 'This could be a bit of a disaster if you're serious about entering the talent contest.'

'Thanks, Hayley,' I replied. 'I'd kinda worked that one out!'

There was a very long silence until Poppy mumbled, 'My big brother Milo can play bass.'

We all looked at each other.

'Pardon?' I said, not sure if I'd heard her properly.

'My brother Milo, in the year above, he's actually pretty good.'

I took a deep breath. This was no ordinary boy. This was Milo Rodgers, the most GORGEOUS BOY ON THE PLANET. Unbelievable!

chapteR six

Sorted?

'Oh God.' I'd just seen a reflection of myself in the café window and my beautifully straightened hair has turned to fuzz. I'd arranged to meet the gorgeous Milo so this was a complete *disaster*.

I still wasn't sure about having a boy in the band but we needed to find someone right now. And you have to look your best if you're going to be seen in public with the coolest boy in school! He was late of course, well he would be or else he wouldn't be the coolest boy in school, would he?

Ten minutes later and I was still sipping a black coffee and beginning to wonder if he'd even turn up. And if he did, what was I going to say to him? I knew I'd need to play it really cool ...

'Tallulah?'

'Yeah?' I turned round and Milo was standing right beside me looking ABSOLUTELY GORGEOUS and wearing a Bee Stings T-shirt. 'Hi. I'm so glad you're here. I thought you weren't

Milo slid into the seat opposite me, his big brown eyes
staring directly at me

coming. We're rehearsing after school tomorrow. Can you make it? We really need you!' It all came blurting out … WHY, OH WHY DID I DO THAT? Seriously uncool! I could feel myself turning from light pink to a deep, rich crimson and I desperately hoped it wasn't too fluorescent.

Milo slid into the seat opposite me, his big brown eyes staring directly at me.

'The thing is, I'm not sure I can. I'm starting my own band and …' he didn't finish the sentence.

I could tell straight away that he basically didn't want to be hanging around with a bunch of girls from the year below. But he's here, so he must be a bit interested. Time for a Tallulah charm offensive.

'Have you got tickets for The Bee Stings gig next Saturday night?' I said as breezily as I could, trying to find a way to get a conversation going.

'Yeah, you goin?'

'Me, yeah.' Which was a lie of course. I wouldn't be allowed to. 'What do you think of the new album?' I continued.

'Oh man, it's awesome. I love that track 'Roller Coaster Casualty' …'

Amazingly, we both immediately started to sing the first line:

♫ *It's the thrill, of the spill,*
that makes a speeding car wreck ♫

We stopped singing and both looked a bit embarrassed. I started giggling, which turned into nervous hysteria and then, miraculously, Milo joined in.

When we eventually stopped laughing, Milo said, 'Are you a bit nuts or what?'

'Maybe just a bit, but please, Milo, we *really* need a bass player for the talent contest and we've already decided on 'Roller Coaster' as our song.'

Milo looked out the window and then back at me. 'OK, as you and Poppy are pals. *But* just till the talent contest, then I'm out.'

Result! I wanted to do some kind of victory dance, but even I realised that would be *too* uncool.

'That's cool, no problem at all,' was the coolest reply I could think of.

'So, Poppy says it's tomorrow at 4,' he said.

'Yeah, that's right.'

Milo sat for a moment, nodded once and then got up and left. AMAZING!

PHEW, we were back on track to win the contest and I started to text the others to let them know we were sorted.

Next morning Patti and I were getting ready for school and I was also putting some clothes together for rehearsals and desperately thinking about how I could get to the Bee Stings gig. I'd decided my skinny black jeans and my Mum's old Siouxsie and the Banshees t-shirt were just right for our first proper rehearsal.

'Patti, will you please let me come to The Bee Stings gig with you next Saturday? Mum said that if I go with you and Gary it's ok.'

I felt like if I could persuade the school heart-throb to join the band I could do anything. I hadn't actually squared it with Mum yet, but I was now determined to and I knew I'd have a better chance if I said Patti and Gary were taking me. I was trying my famous double bluff tactic.

'Where are you going to get a ticket? It's sold out,' Patti replied matter of factly.

'Well, if I can get my hands on a ticket, will you take me?'

'Sure, squirt.'

Patti obviously thought I didn't have a chance of getting one. What she didn't know is that The Bee Stings always hold back some tickets to release only to fan club members the week before the show. And Elizabeth and I had decided we had to go, NO MATTER WHAT. Also I didn't want Milo to think I was a total LOSER if he found out somehow that I was lying about it. Not that I'd care what he thought ... would I?

'Mum said that if I go with you and Gary it's OK'

I headed off to school thinking, roll on 4 o'clock. TALLULAH AND THE TEENSTARS had a rehearsal to go to. And surely nothing else could go wrong now?

I couldn't believe how different my voice sounded

CHAPTER SEVEN

Girls Just Wanna Have Fun

I couldn't believe how different my voice sounded through the PA system at the hall. Gary popped down at the start of the rehearsal to help us set up and put some reverb on my voice, which made it sound all full and sort of dreamy.

Poppy was right about her big bro, he is a really FAB bass player, as well as being drop-dead gorgeous. Just like Poppy, he doesn't say very much but the two of them have a really good groove going. And Hayley and Louisa had obviously been practicing the chords at home for 'Roller Coaster Casualty'. We were sounding so good that I suggested trying another Bee Stings Song, 'Chop Suey Surrender'. WHAT A DISASTER!

I crashed back to earth thinking we really needed to work a bit harder at getting our sound together. Early days though, I suppose. I decided I'd better wait before trying to teach them any of my own songs. But anyway, the first round of the contest was our priority, and for that 'Roller' had to be perfect and it was already sounding pretty decent.

Before we knew it, it was time to pack up and as we did Elizabeth came waltzing in, clearly with something on her mind.

'Guys, image is *so* important. It's one thing sounding good but if you don't look good you might as well forget it.'

Looks like El's on a mission, I thought! She kind of homed in on Poppy and went all Trinny and Su-what's-it, you know those unbearable posh mingers on TV that go around the country telling people to wear more beige stuff. Except Elizabeth was saying Poppy should dye her hair peroxide blonde and lose the orange poncho and flares look.

'I see you in an all-in-one boiler suit, which is right on trend at the moment, maybe in a grey or mint green shiny fabric. That could work brilliantly with your colouring, providing you start wearing make-up of course.'

It was all getting a bit embarrassing so I felt I had to pitch in and take the heat off poor Poppy who looked like she might cry. 'Yeah, I'm going to dye my hair and have it cropped short. I love Jaime Winstone's cut.' Which I did, but I wasn't actually planning on doing it. But I'd said it now. Again! Must remember to try and think before I speak sometimes.

'Listen,' I said. 'Why don't we all get together at my house for a make-over session tomorrow night? My Mum and Dad will be out.' I reckoned some group bonding was a good idea and what better way to do it?

'Are you sure it will be ok with your parents after what happened last time?' Louisa asked.

'YEAH HONESTLY. IT WILL BE TOTALLY COOL,' I said a bit too enthusiastically – obviously trying to convince myself as well as them.

Milo finally spoke. 'Forget it! Count me well and truly out.' Then he left without saying another word, which was becoming a bit of a habit with him.

But the others seemed really keen. Even Poppy, who appeared not to have taken mortal offence to El's lambasting, was up for it.

'It's actually a bit rubbish not having any sisters,' she confessed to us.

'Please have both of mine, they're a *nightmare*,' I replied and we all laughed.

El was ecstatic and said she had some really good style tips for all of us and couldn't wait to get her hands on us. Frankly, I was a bit concerned about what she might have in store for Louisa, as I wasn't sure if she was completely over her hissy fit about her!

I'd told Mum I was having some girlfriends round for a 'study date', which she was over the moon about and even shouted from the front door 'Have fun and don't work *too* hard.' Parents! They really haven't a clue, have they?

I was in the kitchen making mini-pizzas and little sausages on sticks, as I'd decided to do snacks this time. The TeenStars should be here any minute. Elizabeth had come early and straightened my hair to perfection. She arrived with bags of make-up and clothes – I don't know whose wardrobes she'd been raiding – and also a home hair dye kit.

'Elizabeth laid out her make-up brushes next to the biscuits'

'Poppy is quite a challenge,' Elizabeth said as she laid out her make-up brushes next to the biscuits.

'Go easy on her El. I don't want her scared off. I need her.'

'Don't worry, I'll have her looking rock chick gorgeous and she'll be thanking me, just you wait and see, T.'

When the girls arrived, El got straight down to work and Poppy was her very first fashion victim. Nobody had a clue what to expect or if El could really do this at all. She took Poppy away to my bedroom and ages later she was back for the reveal in front of the big hall mirror.

'Oh my God!' Poppy exclaimed, 'I look amazing.'

And by some miracle she really did.

I have to say we were all completely gobsmacked and just stood there with our mouths open. Was it the same girl?!?

El had dyed her mousey hair pure blonde, put false eyelashes on her with lashings of mascara, given her bright red lips, dressed her in an old dress of her Mum's from the 80s and increased her height by about four inches in a pair of black patent knee-length platform boots. I wasn't sure she'd be able to drum in them but otherwise she looked FANTASTIC. Hayley and Louisa actually applauded as she tottered into the room and they

'Oh my God!' Poppy exclaimed, 'I look amazing'

both started to fight about who was next for the 'Eli Le Grande' treatment.

Suddenly it was 10.30 and Poppy's Dad was outside tooting his horn. Everybody was getting ready to leave when Hayley said, 'So Tallulah, when are you having your hair chopped?' Hayley was looking pretty glam in full make up, her hair tonged and dressed in a boy's suit.

'Oh, tomorrow, after rehearsals,' I said. God, I'm really going to have to do it now, I thought.

'You are going to look so COOL with short hair,' Louisa added, looking just the same as when she arrived. Madame Le Grande had run out of time (which I was rather relieved about). And off they went, laughing all the way. What a great night!

I went back in the kitchen to clear up and was thinking what a brilliant band I had. I'd played the girls some of my own songs and they loved them. It really was all coming together. I switched off the kitchen light and was heading up the stairs when there was a really LOUD knock at the front door. I just about jumped out of my skin.

'I KNOW SOMEONE'S IN THERE. OPEN THIS DOOR!' a crazed voice shouted from behind it. 'HAVE YOU SEEN THE STATE OF MY DAUGHTER?'

I was frozen to the spot.

Maggie appeared at the top of the stairs in her pink fluffy dressing gown and face pack, obviously getting ready to go out. 'Answer the door, Teresa. You don't want the whole neighbourhood complaining again after last week,' she half-shouted down at me, trying not to crack her clay face pack, before heading back to her room.

The banging on the front door was getting louder ... I knew I was going to have to answer it.

I opened the door and Poppy and her Mum were standing there. Poppy's Mum looked like she wanted to hit someone – probably me. And to make matters worse my Mum and Dad had just arrived as well and were looking pretty furious.

As usual, my Mum joined in on the shouting, 'Teresa Gordon. What have you been up to now?'

Looked like there might be just a little more trouble ahead ...

chapter eight

Sisters, Such Devoted Sisters

I placed my spare pillow under the duvet and tried to mould it into the best body shape I could. Tip-toeing out my bedroom, I checked that the coast was clear and headed downstairs as quiet as a mouse. I ever so carefully closed the front door behind me and ran down the path and all the way to the bus stop. Phew! Sneaking out the house this morning was a bit trickier than I had expected but there was *no way* I was going to miss

Phew! Sneaking out of the house this morning was a bit trickier than I had expected

rehearsals. I jumped on the bus and texted Poppy to see if she'd made it out alive. She texted back, 'see u there. p x'. I couldn't stop smiling. Nothing could stop us now. Although, last night's drama was still fresh on my mind …

Thank goodness Dad was able to calm everyone down, cos at one point I thought my Mum was going to take a swing at Poppy's Mum when Poppy's Mum said, '*You* might be happy letting your daughter run around looking like a tart but I'm not having it.'

I can't actually remember Mum sticking up for me before. I wanted to hug her. And I couldn't believe Maggie coming to the rescue as well – she made tea for everyone and explained to Poppy's Mum that a dark rinse over the peroxide blonde was all Poppy needed to do to get back to being 'mousey'. The parents managed to iron out their differences over a Hobnob but they still decided to ground us for the weekend. But surely they wouldn't notice us missing so early on a Saturday morning?

I got to the hall and the others were already setting up and chatting away. Well, not Milo obviously, but even a still-blonde Poppy seemed to be coming out of her shell.

Hayley and Louisa were laughing hysterically … 'Oh my God, I can't believe your Mum told Poppy's

Mum to "get a life and, while you're at it, a decent haircut".'

Hayley was gutted she missed the row.

'Yeah, I'm so sorry Poppy. My Mum is a bit mental sometimes.'

'*Your* Mum's mental, what about *mine*? I thought she was going to self-combust,' Poppy said laughing.

'What are you going to do about your hair, Pops?'

'I'm keeping it the way it is, NO MATTER WHAT.' Poppy's new hair colour had given her a whole new attitude.

'What about you, are you still going to get yours done?' Louisa asked me.

'Definitely, but not today, cos after rehearsals I'll have to go straight back home as I'm grounded.'

Then there was a very unexpected interruption ...

'In your own time girls.'

WOW! THE GORGEOUS ONE SPEAKS!

Milo had a point. Every second counted because in less than a week's time we were going to have to take the school talent contest by storm!

By 10.35am, I was back at home. Patti was sitting at the kitchen table eating her usual banana and jam sandwich for breakfast and Mum and Dad had both gone to work.

'Anyone notice me gone Pats?'

'Don't call me that, squirt. No. You're in the clear but if you're not really *really* nice to me today I just might have to tell them. So you can start by doing my chores as well as your own.'

And with that she got up, walked over my toes – a favourite party trick of hers – and headed upstairs for one of her three hour long bubble baths. I decided not to cheese Patti off so I started with her ironing duties cos at least I can listen to my iPod while I do that.

With the early start, rehearsals and all those chores, I was shattered by 6 o'clock and lay down on my bed, strummed the guitar and daydreamed that one day soon my family were going to appreciate me for the talented person I am.

I was just going over in my head my speech for when I win my Ivor Novello songwriting award – you know, the usual sort of thing – 'I'd like to thank my family for all their support and a special thanks to my Mum who ...'

'Teresa Gordon shut that racket up now and come downstairs.'

Mum was home from work. I went down thinking 'I've been rumbled', and I had. Can't seem to get away with anything these days! One of

Mum's customers said she'd seen me with my guitar on the bus this morning and Mum was not happy!

'Listen, Teresa. Ever since you started this band you have been in nothing but trouble. Your Dad and I have been talking and we think you have to give up all this nonsense once and for all. Enough is enough.'

Dad was nodding in agreement all the way through Mum's wee speech. I could feel tears welling up and spilling down my flaming cheeks, 'But Mum ...!'

'No buts. That's it. Tell your friends that's an end to it.'

I WAS ABSOLUTELY HEARTBROKEN. As I started to walk slowly out the door I was just too tired to fight. I hardly even noticed Patti barging past me with Maggie in tow.

'Mum, Dad can we play you something?' Patti said.

'Not now, Patti,' Dad sheepishly replied and without looking at any of us he continued, 'Your Mum and I are in the middle of something.'

But Maggie was already at the CD player inserting a disc. Then the familiar notes of the intro started ... I stopped at the living room door and turned round ...

I hardly even noticed Patti barging past me with Maggie in tow

Feeling like a fool again,
feel I've lost my heart again

My voice came soaring out of the speakers. Mum was just about to say something when Maggie stopped her.

'Please Mum, just listen.' And, for once, she did.

It was the demo I'd recorded with Gary in his home studio. He'd just turned up with it, played it to Patti and Maggie in the kitchen and they decided Mum and Dad needed to hear it as well. Talk about brilliant timing! I hadn't heard the end result before but even I have to admit it sounded pretty good.

A couple of minutes later, the song finished. The Gordon family had a rare moment of silence.

Then my Mum turned to me and said, 'Teresa that was really *good*.'

'Did *you* write that?' Dad asked.

'Ugh hu,' I answered.

And before things went too 'Little House in The Prairie' Patti said, 'Please just let the wee brat have her band. Otherwise she'll make us all suffer with her world class sulking.' Amazing! Patti *never* says please!

With that, Patti headed back to the kitchen where Gary was waiting and Maggie headed upstairs – after all, she only had another four hours to get ready before she went clubbing.

I sat down feeling a bit teary and told Mum and Dad all about the talent contest and everything. And, amazingly, they said that as long as I stayed out of trouble I could stay in the band.

Then I had a thought. 'Mum, you wouldn't cut my hair after tea, would you?'

'Do you really think it's OK, El?'

Chapter Nine

Please Don't Laugh ...

I was standing in the girls' toilet looking at myself (again!) in the smudged mirror. 'Do you really think it's ok, El?' I asked for the thousandth time that week as I moved my head from side to side, checking my new bob was sitting perfectly.

'It's FAB, but if you ask me one more time, I might have to stick your head down the loo and FLUSH it.'

'Sorry, it's just I'm a bit nervous about the contest on Friday. I really, really want us to get through.' As I finished speaking Ava Smart and Mia MacIntyre walked in – they are in the year above us and everybody secretly wants to be them. They are gorgeous, really cool in a cutesy way and boys think they are very funny. Girls don't, (unless they are part of their exclusive gang). El and I are a bit nervous of them, not that they had ever talked to us or anything. Until that moment ...

Ava Smart and Mia MacIntyre walked in

'Are you Teresa Gordon?' Mia moved towards me and I found myself stepping backwards.

'Yes,' I tried to say as casually as I could while retreating.

'Is it true that you've entered your band in the talent contest?'

'Ye-es,' I said hesitantly.

'So you're Tallulah?'

'Yes,' I said, wondering if I should have said no as I had no idea where this conversation was heading.

'And what about titch? Is she in the band?'

'No, but I'm the band's official stylist,' El said squaring up to Ava.

Mia and Ava burst out laughing and Ava looked at me with a mixture of disbelief and disgust and said, 'This we *have* to see'. And then they disappeared into a toilet cubicle together still laughing uncontrollably.

El and I made a fast exit without saying a word until we were all the way down the corridor. I felt sick. It looked like everyone would know pretty soon that boring old Teresa Gordon was Tallulah Gosh and everybody in school would be there to LAUGH at us.

'Look, don't worry about those two mingers, T. They haven't got a clue. I mean, come on, they still think *High School Musical* is cool.'

I nodded my head in agreement but was beginning to feel pretty wobbly about the whole thing. There was only one more rehearsal and that was today after school.

'Yeah, see you after English,' I managed to say as I headed off upstairs to class.

What a day. Rehearsals were actually fine and as soon as we started playing I lost the sick feeling that had stayed with me all afternoon. And I couldn't believe that Milo said he liked my hair. In fact, he kept looking at me and then turning away, or maybe I just imagined that. We had a final styling session with El after rehearsals which went well – if nothing else, I thought, people would be amazed by our 'out of uniform' look. I decided not to tell the others about Ava and Mia just in case it put them off. Of course nobody dared ask Milo what he was going to wear, he always looked good.

I was already in bed when Patti came into our room.

'Are you coming tomorrow?' I asked.

'Coming where?'

I knew she was just pretending that she didn't know what I meant.

'The contest!'

'Oh, that. Course I am squirt.' She switched her

bedside lamp on to read just as I was turning mine off – yip, sharing a room can be pretty annoying.

I woke up really early. The big day had finally arrived. I couldn't face breakfast and Mum didn't force it but she handed me a banana and an extra big sandwich as I was leaving and said, 'Just be yourself and you'll do fine. And at least eat your banana cos you can't do anything if you don't have the energy.' Good old Mum!

I couldn't wait for 2 o'clock to arrive and the start of the contest. My stomach was in knots. Then suddenly it was time.

There were twelve acts in the contest. Tallulah and the TeenStars were ninth on the bill so we had lots of time to get panicky backstage and we seemed to be falling apart. I managed to break two guitar strings while tuning my guitar. Hayley forgot her lucky duck that sat on her keyboard and was on the verge of a nervous breakdown about it until she discovered it was in her pocket. Louisa arrived red faced and just in the nick of time because her teacher had kept her back and she'd had to run the whole way. Act 7 started, a dance troupe from our year called 'Happy Feet'. Poppy and Milo were still totally calm which helped all of us to relax just a bit and I even managed to eat my banana.

No wonder we were nervous. Only the top six acts would get through to the final the following week and it was up to the audience to decide who was best.

Mr Forsyth, the Head of Drama, popped his head round the door. 'OK, Teresa and the TeenStars, get ready, Sonny's just started.'

Sonny Brady from the year below was on just before us. He had a magic act and even had a real live mouse for it.

'It's *Tallulah* and the TeenStars, Mr Forsyth,' Milo said as he moved closer to me and squeezed my hand. I don't know why I felt amazing after that, but I did. We were standing in the wings waiting and I peeped out to see the audience. It looked like the whole school had come and they were Oohing and Ahhing at Sonny's incredible tricks. I spotted Sir Acne No-mates down the front; he had been on earlier doing a 'French Horn' solo, which I didn't catch but someone back stage had described as 'brilliantly BAD'.

Then, suddenly, it was our turn and Mr Forsyth stepped on stage to announce us. We had been allowed to set up our equipment at lunchtime at the back of the stage behind the Fire Curtain to save time. So we were all sorted, amps were on, keyboards checked, mics on, guitars tuned. I felt

Milo squeezed my hand - I felt amazing!

pretty good in the turquoise sequined mini-dress
that El said had been her Gran's in the 60's. In fact
all the TeenStars looked great. I couldn't help but
think we really did look like a proper band and
hoped Patti would remember to take some pics.

We were as ready as we'd ever be ...

The curtain was only halfway up when I turned to Poppy and yelled 1,2,3,4. I couldn't wait a second longer for this moment to begin.

Boy we were LOUD! I stepped forward to the microphone and sang my heart out, as the band played the song with total tantalising conviction. It was over in a flash but I knew we ROCKED! But, I had been too lost in the joy of it to notice until the end that the entire school were on their feet. I stood looking out smiling, my body was shivering and I just really wanted to stay on stage and do it all over again.

When we left the stage it was to the sound of feet stomping, cheering and whistling.

'That's enough noise,' a now harassed Mr Forsyth pleaded with the audience. He was waving his arms around in an attempt to retain some order in the erupted school hall. Elizabeth was waiting for us backstage, jumping up and down squeaking, 'You were brilliant, absolutely brilliant. Even Ava Smart-Ass and Mia Marvellous were cheering at the end – did you see?'

Then Patti arrived with her friend Flora, 'You did OK little sis, I've got some great shots.'

WOW! A compliment from Patti – I couldn't believe it!

I was still tingling with excitement as I turned to

Boy we were LOUD!

the TeenStars and said, 'OK, what on earth are we going to do next week?'

I knew there was no way we weren't getting through to the next round, not after that reaction!

chaPTeR TeN

Rock'n'Roll

Patti, Gary and I were standing at Boots' Corner, huddled under a polka dot umbrella, waiting for Elizabeth. And it seemed the whole town had decided to meet here. We were off to see Betty and the Bee Stings and I should have been really excited – but I just wasn't. I was totally bummed and nearly didn't come. The rain was hopping off the ground and it was freezing and I'd had a clothes crisis, and my feet hurt in these stupid high heels and everything was just completely WRONG.

'Come on Tallulah,' Gary said. 'You'll figure something out.'

'I doubt it,' I replied.

'If Elizabeth doesn't get here in the next two minutes, we're going without her,' Patti, the Queen of Strops, declared.

We had easily been the most popular act in the contest but the Head decided we were just too loud and we were not going to be allowed to take part in the final. She said how much she regretted her decision but that, 'it was just not suitable for this type of school exercise.'

School exercise! What does that mean? It was a talent contest. And don't you hate it when parents and teachers say they 'regret the decision'. WELL DON'T MAKE IT.

El turned up in a canary yellow shiny mac with gold buttons and we all headed off to Tiffany's. There was a massive queue all around the block but I spotted Milo near the front although I couldn't see who he was with. I waved but he didn't see me.

We slowly made our way up the queue and despite the rain and all the wrongs in my life I began to feel a tiny twinge of excitement.

The only other gig I had been to see was The SugaBabes and my Mum had insisted on taking me. It was actually pretty good apart from my Mum's really embarrassing dancing. She looked like she was having some kind of fit.

'Please T, don't let what happened yesterday spoil tonight – I know it's rubbish what the Head did, she is completely out of order but you've still got a band and NOBODY can take that away from you.'

El was absolutely right and I hugged her. Tonight was going to be special no matter what.

We finally made it into Tiffany's and it was

heaving with people. Patti shouted over the noise of the crowd, 'OK, you two, stand outside the girls' loos at the end and we'll come and get you,' and with that they disappeared into the huge crowd.

El and I decided to get as near to the front as we could and had to twist and turn our way through till finally we squeezed into a tiny space three rows from the front. The support band was pretty good – two boys and two girls called Candyfloss Martyrs. They certainly got the crowd going and everyone was bouncing up and down. Then I spotted Milo at the front of the balcony. Unbelievable! He was with Ava Smart! Surely he couldn't be with Ava Smart? I could hardly believe my eyes. I pointed them out to El and she looked at me with total amazement and shouted into my ear, 'What a FREAK.' I didn't know why I felt so strange about it but decided I was going to completely ignore them if I saw them.

'I didn't know they were friends?' I bellowed at El.

'Looks like they are more than friends!' El replied and pointed up to them. He had his arm around her. Ugh! 'What a pair of LOSERS!' El said and hugged me again. El was very excited.

Everyone started chanting BETTY, BETTY. Then it went really dark for a minute before there was a flash of brilliant light and the band sent the

The band sent the crowd wild by opening with 'School Hurts The Best'

crowd wild by opening with 'School Hurts The Best'. They played an amazing set and did *three* encores.

IT WAS THE BEST NIGHT I'VE EVER HAD. I was tingling all over, it was as if electricity had entered my body and made me feel more alive than I had ever been. And I realised that one day I wanted Tallulah and the TeenStars to play Tiffany's just like the Bee Stings. Who cares what our pathetic Head thinks and who cares about the Mias and the Avas of the world. I felt absolutely brilliant and one day I was going to play alongside Betty – I just knew it.

El and I had been separated in the sudden rush to get out and I was being pushed to the back of the hall. I kept standing on my tiptoes trying to find El but I just couldn't see her anywhere. But she knew the meeting place.

'Try her on her mobile again, Tee,' Patti suggested – she was never going to call me Tallulah I realised.

We'd been waiting around 15 mins and I was beginning to get worried, but I didn't say so.

I left another message for her just as Milo and Ava approached. Oh God, what was I going to do now?

Milo and Ava approached

'Hi,' Milo manages.

'Wasn't it FAB!' Ava gushes.

I nodded.

'Oh, and by the way, I LOVED your band yesterday. Milo hadn't even told me he was in it. But you guys were really cool.'

I was stunned, I even suspected she meant it.

'Th .. thanks,' I stuttered out.

'Oh yeah, and Mia and I have started a petition,' Ava added.

'What pet ...'

Just then, El suddenly appeared and stopped me asking my question.

'You are never going to believe who I just met. BILLY CHAINSAW!' Billy Chainsaw runs the *official* Bee Stings Fan Club!

'Look, I don't care if you met Betty herself, we are going to miss the last bus home if you don't get a move on.' Patti was in charge and she was right. We needed to get home – none of us needed any more parental meltdowns.

We said goodbye and headed off and for some reason I couldn't help feeling that everything was going to be OK. And not just because it had finally stopped raining.

ChAPTeR eLeVeN

Just Be Yourself

I thought I might pass out with boredom during double Maths, but at least lunchtime was next. I'd called a band meeting in the cold lunch corridor to discuss our next move. Tallulah and the TeenStars were not over just because we'd been barred from the stupid school talent contest. In fact I'd decided that I thought it's pretty cool that we had. (Of course Mum and Dad wanted to know what we did wrong! Phew, parents – are they *ever* on your side?) The bell rang and I was collecting my stuff together when Mr Band, the school secretary, appeared at the door and called my name:

'Teresa Gordon, the Head wants to see you in her office,' he said casually.

I froze. I'd never even been in the Head's office before and I certainly didn't want to go now.

'Hurry up Teresa, she wants to see you now.'

I staggered out of class trying very hard to look like I wasn't bothered. So what? The head wanted to see me? I was wondering if I should do a runner and pretend I didn't get the message.

I knocked on the door and waited to be told to come in ... I felt a bit ill.

'Enter.'

I walked in slowly and couldn't decide whether I should sit down or not and where, cos there were lots of seats.

'Sit down Teresa, please, or should I call you Tallulah?' she said, smiling at me.

I didn't manage to answer but I managed to sit down on the chair furthest away from her desk. She continued ...

'It would appear the whole school wants to see you perform again, judging by the online petition I've received and the non-stop badgering from the staff.' And off she went on a very long ramble ...

By the time I got to the cold lunch corridor, word had got out that I had been sent for. Everyone was whispering and looking at me as I made my way through to my usual seat. Even Milo had turned up.

Elizabeth stood up when she saw me, 'Everything OK T?'

'Yip, I'm fine ... the Head said I could take part in the final. But without the band.'

'What, just you – no TeenStars?' El asked.

'Yes, she said it would be less noisy that way and more manageable. And that there had been a petition and she was looking for a compromise and if I just sang on my own and she went on and on ...' my sentence trailed off.

Hayley, Poppy, Milo and El looked at me.

'But I said no, told her we are a BAND and that was that.'

Nobody said anything, so I sat down and pulled my cheese sandwiches out of my bag and started to munch as quietly as I could.

Hayley broke the silence, 'Are you sure T? I mean, you could probably win.'

Then Poppy added, 'T, you've got to do it on your own. We know how much this means to you.'

'Look, guys, I've made up my mind ... we play together or not at all.'

The bell went and lunchtime came to an end. I wished I could just go home but now I had to endure French and Physics – I really don't like Mondays.

My school day eventually dragged to an end and I found myself standing at the bus stop feeling numb about the day's events. I was listening to my iPod when I felt a hand on my shoulder. I turned round ... I couldn't believe it was Ava and Mia. This was all I needed.

'Listen, Tallulah, Milo just told us about you and the Head,' Mia said.

'Mmm,' I replied.

'Not many people would take a stand like that,' Ava added.

I couldn't really think of anything more to say about it. People had been asking me all afternoon. So I said nothing.

'Look, Tallulah, have you ever seen *MTV Unplugged*? It's when a band play their songs acoustically, no amps, no drums ... they do it a bit differently ... and we ...'

'Yeah, I know.'

'Well, maybe THAT could be the compromise.' Ava and Mia were both smiling at me and I smiled back. BRILLIANT!!! Now why didn't I think of that?

'But, I've already told the Head it's a no.'

'Don't worry about that, we'll petition her again, leave it to us. We've got Mr Forsyth on our side as well,' Mia concluded.

I suddenly realised Ava and Mia are the coolest girls in school for good reason. And, I absolutely knew we could do an amazing 'unplugged' job of my song 'Feet First'.

ALL OF US, TOGETHER. TALLULAH AND THE TEENSTARS. YEAH! YEAH! YEAH!

CHAPTER TWELVE

We Rule!

I was as happy as a girl can be ... I'd just had a mug of hot chocolate and a pineapple cake. I was lying on my bed on top of the covers, my legs were all tingly and I couldn't stop moving them around. And I couldn't stop re-playing in my head what had happened that afternoon either.

We were on second this time and although I was nervous I couldn't wait to get back on stage. It's funny cos the thought of performing in front of lots of people terrifies me but as soon as I start playing my guitar and singing I feel completely at home ... almost like a different person. Still me but even more me ... like a bigger, bolder me ... it's hard to describe.

Working out how to do the song the new way took a while but once we figured it out it sounded better and better. Mum and Dad even let us have an extra rehearsal in the garage! I couldn't believe it when I asked them and they actually said yes. It was a monumental moment for me – Mum and Dad know the word YES and they said it to me! HOORAY!

Poppy played bongos, Louisa and Milo still had their first ever guitars which were acoustic so they played them and Hayley played her violin which was the first instrument she'd ever learned. She said she'd stopped playing it cos other kids used to laugh at her. But it sounded brilliant and it really worked with the melody. I just sang. Which was a bit weird at the start but it was lovely to be able to concentrate on my singing. I thought at first our performance wasn't going down so well because people were sitting pretty quietly, not really dancing or anything. I guess they were just listening cos at the end the whole school went absolutely crazy! Obviously, having Milo in the band helps but even so, they really liked us – ALL OF US – and we won!

The Head described us as 'most unusual' before awarding us our book tokens. Milo didn't want his, so he gave it to Poppy and I couldn't help but think what a nice big brother to have. Hayley and Louisa couldn't stop laughing when Sir Acne No-Mates turned up backstage to ask for auto-graphs and El was selling T-shirts with our name in BIG BOLD letters that she'd made. I think 'Happy

Feet', who ended up coming in second, were not so happy about us winning. In fact, they seemed well cheesed off. I heard one of them say 'it's not even a proper contest, not like *Britain's Got Talent* or anything'. I didn't care what they thought … I just wanted us to do our song well and for people to like it. And we did and they did. In fact it was the most amazing feeling in the world – people liking us. My head was spinning with excitement when the Head announced us as the winners. What a day!

'OK Miss Tallulah Gosh, switch that light off and get some sleep, it's one o'clock in the morning, you know.' Mum was on her way to bed and popped in to give me an update on what I was doing wrong but at least she got the name right – at last!

'And, don't think for a second just cos you won a talent contest at school it lets you off doing the dishes. That dishwasher won't pack itself!' I'd been too busy on the phone with the rest of the TeenStars to do my chores!

'Yeah Mum, I'll get up early and do it.'

'Don't worry, it's done.' Mum sat down on the end of my bed.

'Well done Teresa, I heard you were great today. Now get some beauty sleep – YOU need it.' She laughed and gave me a big hug and went off to smother herself in her usual variety of night time lotions and potions. And I switched my lamp off wondering what on earth was going to happen next?

Well, nothing happened next. School the next week was a total drag. Monday was quite exciting with lots of people talking to us about winning and stuff but by Tuesday nobody seemed that bothered about us. I mean, I think I was no longer completely invisible in people's eyes but everything just went back to normal. And by Thursday it was like it had never happened. El and I were walking to the bus stop at home time and we both felt a bit fed up and we didn't really know why.

'You know what El, I need more in life than double art to look forward to.'

'Mmm, me too. Are you rehearsing tonight?' El asked.

'Yeah, but I'm not sure what for, we don't have anywhere to perform. We need another contest or some proper gigs or … I dunno.'

'Don't worry T, all bands face a struggle at the start.'

I got on the bus and headed to rehearsals feeling completely flat and flatter still when I realised that

I got on the bus and headed to rehearsals feeling completely flat

nobody else had arrived yet. I was strumming my guitar and writing a new song in my head called 'What's The Point' when I got a text from El.

WILL MEET U AFTER I FINISH WORK. GOT SOME V. EXCITING NEWS.

I reckoned she'd got that sewing machine she was after on eBay.

Eventually the others turned up and we just mucked around a bit. It was actually pretty good fun but I could tell the TeenStars were all wondering where *do* we go from here?

We were having a thrash at the old Sex Pistols classic 'Pretty Vacant' when El suddenly burst into the hall.

'Guys, I have some amazing news for you!' She paused and then shouted at the top of her voice, 'BETTY AND THE BEE STINGS WANT YOU TO SUPPORT THEM ON TOUR THIS SUMMER.'

'WHAT …?' Looked like El had really lost the plot this time!

'I just spoke to Billy Chainsaw – he phoned me. The night of their gig, when I lost you, I gave him a tape of you guys in the talent contest doing 'Roller Coaster'. I shot it on my Mum's DVD camera and you know the demo you did with Gary. Well Billy played them to Betty and she loves it and wants you to open the shows for them in July. All ten of them.'

We all just looked at each other, our mouths open ...

'Are you *sure* about this, Elizabeth?' Louisa asked.

'Yeah, absolutely! He said you need to get your manager to call their manager and they can sort out details and stuff.'

'But we don't have a manager,' Poppy couldn't help but point out our first hurdle.

'But you can get one. I bet Gary would do it.' El was answering questions and already thinking outfits and I was standing listening to everyone talking all at once and I couldn't quite believe it but I also thought, this is it ... and I started babbling ...

'WOW, this is the best thing ever, this is so so cool, it's unbelievable, it's amazing, it's just brilliant ... Oh my God ... oh my God ... oh my God, what are our parents going to say?'

Suddenly the room went silent and, eventually, Hayley quietly said what we were all thinking ...

'They are *never* going to let us.'

Milo cleared his throat and added, 'Yeah, I think she might have a point, I mean they wouldn't even let Poppy go and see them last time they played.'

We all looked at Poppy and she was standing with her hands on her hips, shaking her head and looking like she might cry with frustration and anger and the sheer injustice of being fourteen and 'not allowed'.

Then something came over me …

'LISTEN, there is no way we can let any of our parents stop us. I don't care what it takes or how we do it. This is our big chance and we have to make it happen. We have to, we just do. And I'm not sure how but TALLULAH AND THE TEENSTARS will tour this summer. I mean COME ON we need to prove to everyone that we are a proper band and not just a bunch of school kids. This is our actual CHANCE to live our DREAM.' I stopped there …

I have to confess at this point I really had no idea how I was going to get our parents to say yes but I knew I could. I'm TALLULAH GOSH and I could make it happen cos I know that dreams can come true. You just sometimes have to work harder at them than you think to make them REAL. And I knew we could do that. I started laughing and I wanted to hug people but I resisted cos they were already looking at me like I was NUTS.

'Let's play 'Roller Coaster Casualty',' I said, lifted up my beautiful guitar, the others grabbed their instruments and I yelled 1,2,3,4 … the only numbers I TRULY LOVE. And I just know everything will be OK, cos we are TALLULAH AND THE TEENSTARS, YEAH! YEAH! YEAH!

'LISTEN, there is no way we can let any of our parents stop us'

The End

But look for book 2 of *The Adventures of Tallulah Gosh* TALLULAH ON TOUR. Available soon at all good bookstores and online at amazon.co.uk.